THE EMPTY POT

DEMI

A TRUMPET CLUB SPECIAL EDITION

For
Tze-Si
Jesse
Huang

Published by The Trumpet Club
666 Fifth Avenue, New York, New York 10103

Copyright © 1990 by Demi

ISBN 0-440-84476-2

This edition published by arrangement with
Henry Holt and Company, Inc.

Designed by Maryann Leffingwell

Printed in the United States of America
January 1992

10 9 8 7 6 5 4 3 2 1
UPR

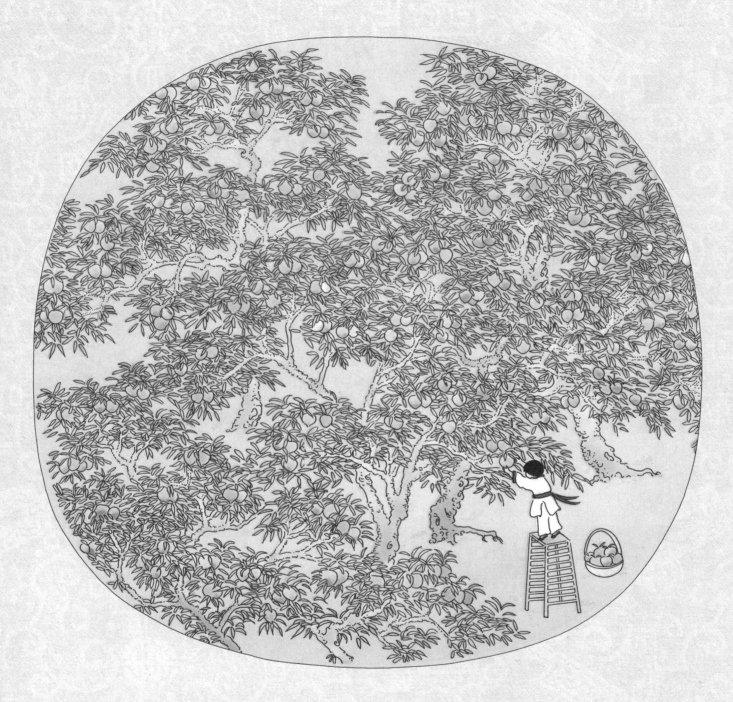

A long time ago in China there was a boy named Ping who loved flowers. Anything he planted burst into bloom. Up came flowers, bushes, and even big fruit trees, as if by magic!

Everyone in the kingdom loved flowers too.

They planted them everywhere, and the air smelled like perfume.

The Emperor loved birds and animals, but flowers most of all,
and he tended his own garden every day.

But the Emperor was very old. He needed to choose a successor
to the throne.

Who would his successor be? And how would the Emperor choose? Because the Emperor loved flowers so much, he decided to let the flowers choose.

The next day a proclamation was issued: All the children in the land were to come to the palace. There they would be given special flower seeds by the Emperor. "Whoever can show me their best in a year's time," he said, "will succeed me to the throne."

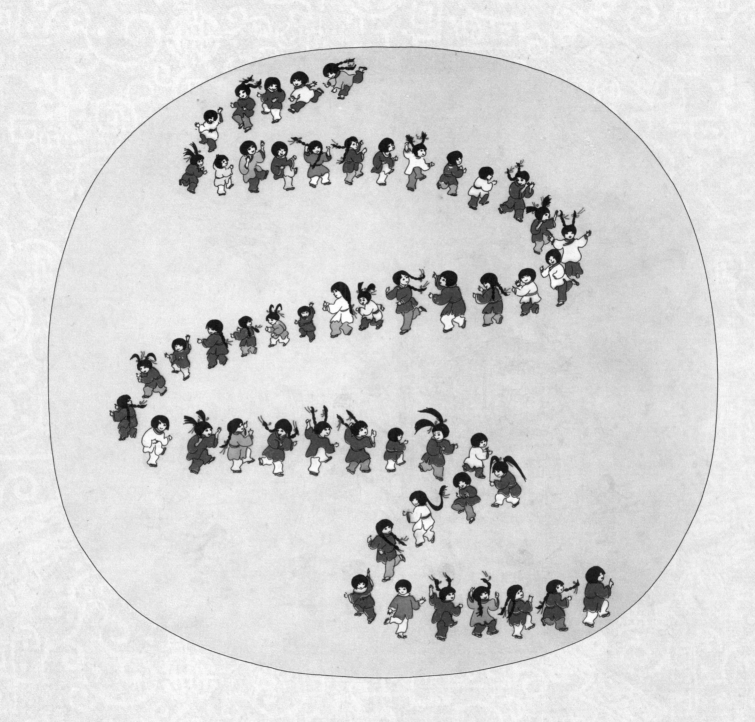

This news created great excitement throughout the land! Children from all over the country swarmed to the palace to get their flower seeds.

All the parents wanted their children to be chosen Emperor, and all the children hoped they would be chosen too!

When Ping received his seed from the Emperor, he was the happiest child of all. He was sure he could grow the most beautiful flower.

Ping filled a flowerpot with rich soil. He planted the seed in it very carefully.

He watered it every day. He couldn't wait to see it sprout, grow, and blossom into a beautiful flower!

Day after day passed, but nothing grew in his pot.

Ping was very worried. He put new soil into a bigger pot.

Then he transferred the seed into the rich black soil.

Another two months he waited. Still nothing happened.

By and by the whole year passed.

Spring came, and all the children put on their best clothes to greet the Emperor.

They rushed to the palace with their beautiful flowers, eagerly hoping to be chosen.

Ping was ashamed of his empty pot. He thought the other children would laugh at him because for once he couldn't get a flower to grow.

His clever friend ran by, holding a great big plant. "Ping!" he said. "You're not really going to the Emperor with an empty pot, are you? Couldn't you grow a great big flower like mine?"

"I've grown lots of flowers better than yours," Ping said. "It's just this seed that won't grow."

Ping's father overheard this and said, "You did your best, and
your best is good enough to present to the Emperor."

Holding the empty pot in his hands, Ping went straight away
to the palace.

The Emperor was looking at the flowers slowly, one by one.

How beautiful all the flowers were!
But the Emperor was frowning and did not say a word.

Finally he came to Ping. Ping hung his head in shame, expecting to be punished.

The Emperor asked him, "Why did you bring an empty pot?"

Ping started to cry and replied, "I planted the seed you gave me and I watered it every day, but it didn't sprout. I put it in a better pot with better soil, but still it didn't sprout! I tended it all year long, but nothing grew. So today I had to bring an empty pot without a flower. It was the best I could do."

When the Emperor heard these words, a smile slowly spread over his face, and he put his arm around Ping. Then he exclaimed to one and all, "I have found him! I have found the one person worthy of being Emperor!

"Where you got your seeds from, I do not know. For the seeds I gave you had all been cooked. So it was impossible for any of them to grow.

"I admire Ping's great courage to appear before me with the empty truth, and now I reward him with my entire kingdom and make him Emperor of all the land!"